Tales of Fairies and Elves

CONTENTS

Exeter Books

NEW YORK

The Fairies' Cake

"Oh, we'll turn you into a tree."

"I don't want to turn into a tree," thought Lucy. So she said to the fairies, "How can I make a cake without flour? You'd better fly to my kitchen and fetch me a bag of flour."

So the fairies flitted over to the croft where Lucy lived, and flitted back with a bag of flour.

Lucy shook her head. "How can I make a cake without eggs? You'd better fly me to my hen-house and fetch me half a dozen eggs."

So the fairies flew over to the hen-house, and flew back with half a dozen eggs.

"But how can I make a cake without sugar?" said Lucy to the fairies. "You'd better hurry to my cupboard and fetch a bag of sugar." So the fairies fluttered over to the croft and found in the cupboard a bag of sugar, and

There was once a young lady called Lucy who baked the best cakes in the whole world. One day she was stolen away by the fairies, who locked her up in the kitchen in Fairyland. "Make us a cake!" they all demanded. "A big, gooey, crumbly, creamy cake with icing!"

"And what will become of me when I've done baking?" asked Lucy.

between them carried it back to Fairyland. "Och, but you forgot the baking powder!" cried Lucy. "Do you want a cake as flat as a dinner plate?" And she sent the fairies back for the baking powder. She sent them for the icing sugar, the cherries, the cream and a bowl. And with every trip the fairies grew more and more tired, until their wings drooped. "There! I'm ready!" said Lucy, putting all the ingredients into the bowl. "But oh dear, I'm too worried about my poor wee baby to think about cake-making. You must go and fetch him for me to watch over while I cook."

"Oh, all right," said the fairies grudgingly. They did not want to go — they were worn out. But how else could they get their cake?

They were no sooner back, carrying the baby in his crib, than Lucy looked at her watch. "Oh goodness gracious! It's time for my husband's tea. I must go home and cook him something."

"Oh no you don't!" said the fairies. "Let him make his own tea!" But Lucy fell into such fits of giggles that she could neither whisk nor stir. "Make his own tea? Why, he couldn't butter a slice of bread! Oh, no, you must fetch him so I can explain why his tea's late."

a cake more than ever. So they folded their wings across their backs and walked all the way over to Lucy's croft, and carried back the cat and the dog.

"Now. At last I'm ready to bake the cake," said Lucy. "But where's the oven?"

"Oven?" The fairies began to grizzle. "Do you need an oven?"

Lucy laughed and her husband laughed, too. "Of course I need an oven!"

So the fairies crawled over to the croft and staggered back under the gigantic weight of the cast-iron kitchen range.

While they were gone, Lucy said to her husband, "Sing!" And she said to the cat, "Yowl!" And she said to the dog,

So the fairies flapped over to the croft — and flapped back with Lucy's husband. Then they sat back to back on the floor to catch their breath.

"Did you lock up the cat and dog before you left?" Lucy asked her husband sharply — though she winked an eye as she spoke.

"Er . . . er, no, I-I didn't have time."

"What? The dog and cat not locked up? Why, they'll scratch the house to pieces! You fairies will have to fetch them here — no two ways about it!"

The fairies could hardly bring themselves to get up off the floor. But they were so hungry that they wanted

"Ssh! Oh shush! Stop!" shrieked the fairies, covering their ears. "Go away, *please!*" they cried, pulling their pillows over their heads.

"Very well," said Lucy. "But only if you promise to fetch my oven home tomorrow morning at the latest."

Then her husband picked up the baby in his crib, and Lucy picked up the cat, and the dog followed on behind. They walked home to a meal of cold pork pie and toasted crumpets.

But Lucy, though she had narrowly escaped being turned into a tree, felt

"Bark!" And she said to the baby, "Cry!"

The door flew open, and in came the oven. The fairies set it down, then sprawled on their little fairy beds, exhausted.

But the man was singing.
And the cat was yowling.
And the dog was barking.
And the baby was crying.

sorry for the fairies with no-one to bake them cakes. So when they brought back her oven, the first thing she did was to bake a big, gooey, crumbly, creamy cake with icing on top, and she left it outside the door. And do you know what? Next morning it was gone.

THE DANCING FAIRIES

Once upon a time, on the Swedish island of Göv, there lived a servant called Little Anders. He worked as a groom in the stables of Mr Strale, the clergyman. Now Little Anders was a dreamer. He dreamed all day and all night about elves and fairies, and he often fell asleep when he was supposed to be working. And, one hot Midsummer's Day, he slept right through the afternoon.

"Wake up, Little Anders," said his master. "It's late! Hurry down to the meadow and fetch my horse. We must lock him up safely before dark or the fairies will whisk him away."

The full Midsummer moon was shining brightly by the time Little Anders reached the meadow. Suddenly he heard the strangest music from far above his head. Then, as he listened, a cloud of winged fairies sailed down a moonbeam and landed in the middle of a circle of dark grass, where they danced to the music of a fairy orchestra. Leading them was their Queen, who was taller than the others and very beautiful. She wore a silver crown and her dress sparkled with precious stones.

Little Anders crept closer and closer to watch. Then the Queen called out: "Stop! There's a stranger present!" The music ceased, and the dancers stood like statues. "You'd better go home," said the Queen, turning to Little Anders. "Or you may find yourself bewitched."

"I'd rather dance with you," he replied, and no sooner had he spoken than he found himself in the middle of the fairy ring, with the Queen in his arms.

They danced for hours, but then the Queen cried out: "Stop! It's almost cock-crow. It's time we were back in Fairyland!" And the fairies flew off, leaving poor Anders dancing by himself.

His master found him there in the morning, still dancing. He danced all the way home, and he danced up and down the stairs. He danced all day and he danced all night. Indeed, he danced for three whole days!

Then, nearly a month later, on the night of the full moon, Little Anders climbed out of his window just before midnight and ran all the way to the meadow. Once again he heard the wonderful music and saw the fairy dancers sailing through the sky, led by their Queen. This time she seemed more beautiful than ever.

Folding their wings, they all began dancing with Anders and the Queen in the centre of the fairy ring. And, as before, they danced happily until dawn. Then the Queen said: "Stop! It's almost cock-crow and must be off. Goodbye, Little Anders. Hurry home."

"No!" shouted Anders. "This time I'm going with you!" And, clutching the Queen's robe, he sailed with her up a moonbeam and into the sky, the other fairies following behind.

But this was not the last of Little Anders. Old Mr Strale told everyone that on Midsummer Nights, when the moon was full, he would see Anders dancing in the meadow. From midnight until cock-crow, circled round by all the winged creatures of Fairyland, he danced in the arms of the beautiful fairy Queen.

SCARLET BRACES

Now if there's one thing the people of Ireland know about, it's the ways of the Irish leprechaun. They will tell you that the leprechauns make all the shoes and boots the fairies wear. They will tell you that every leprechaun has a pot of gold hidden away in a secret place. And they will tell you, if you see a leprechaun, never to take your eyes off him or he will disappear before you look back again.

That is why, when Pat Fitzpatrick went out and about each day, he was always saying to himself, "If I ever see a leprechaun, I won't take my eyes off him till he gives me his pot of gold."

Pat might have been a better boy if he had spent more time helping his mother dig potatoes and less time looking for leprechauns and pots of gold.

Still, all that searching paid off. One fine day Pat caught sight of a little man — no bigger than his own hand — sitting on a toadstool, sewing a pair of fairy boots. Pat bit his lip and stood very still. "I won't take my eyes off him, so I won't. Not till he's made me the richest boy in all Ireland!"

Quietly, Pat crept through the grass until he was close enough to reach out and grab the leprechaun in his fist.

"Got you! Now, where's your pot of gold?"

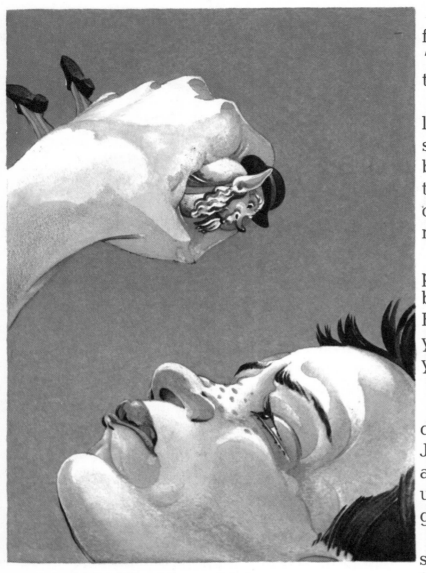

free and could point over Pat's shoulder. "Look, boy, and be quick! Your cow's in the corn!"

Pat very nearly turned his head to look. But, just in the nick of time, he saw it was a trick. "You'll have to do better than that," he laughed, shaking the leprechaun. "I am not taking my eyes off you till I have your pot of gold safe in my hands!"

Then the leprechaun burst into pitiful tears. "Ah, you're a cruel, heartless boy, so you are. Anyone can see that: Here you stand talking of gold when your own house is burning down and your mother inside it!"

"What!"

In his horror, Pat very nearly dropped the leprechaun and ran home. Just in the nick of time, he saw it was a trick, and shook the leprechaun until the poor little fellow turned as green as his own coat.

"All right, all right," the leprechaun spluttered at last. "I'll tell you where to find my pot of gold."

"Oh! Would you frighten a poor creature half to death?" cried the leprechaun, and his little heart pounded beneath Pat's fingers. "What's that you say about gold? I don't know of any gold, or anything about it at all!"

Pat squeezed the leprechaun a little tighter, never once looking away. "Don't give me any of your nonsense, now," he said. "I shan't let you go until you show me your pot of gold."

The leprechaun writhed and struggled until he wriggled one hand

from round the leprechaun and tied them round the thistle instead, to mark it. Then he pushed the leprechaun deep into his pocket.

But the very moment he lost sight of him, the leprechaun changed into thin air and was gone.

Pat did not mind. He ran home as fast as his legs would carry him, and fetched a spade. It was so heavy that he had to drag it behind him all the way back to the hill. "Thought he could trick me, eh?" he panted. "Well, he didn't reckon on the cleverness of good old Pat

"No you won't, you'll show me the very spot," said Pat. And taking off his scarlet braces, he tied them to the leprechaun like a lead to a dog.

The magical little cobbler led Pat to the top of a hill. Thousands upon thousands of thistles grew in every direction. He stopped beside one thistle that looked exactly like every other.

"Since you won't take your eyes off me, I am unable to tell you a lie. My pot of gold's buried below this particular thistle. But I'm thinking you'll need a spade if you're to dig it up."

"Oho, I see your trick," Pat jeered, squeezing the leprechaun until the little chap's eyes bulged. "You think I'll never find this one thistle again among so many!" So he untied the scarlet braces

Fitzpatrick!"

Puffing and blowing, he stopped at the top of the hill to mop his forehead. And there was a sight in front of him that made his jaw drop.

A pair of scarlet braces dangled from every thistle in sight, as far as the eye could see — thousands upon thousands of scarlet braces. There was no more hope of recognising the leprechaun's thistle than of finding one particular drop of water in the whole of the Irish Sea.

So, if you ever chance to see a leprechaun, and you've a mind to steal his pot of gold, you had better keep a sharp eye on the little fellow . . . and remember the story of Pat Fitzpatrick and his scarlet braces!

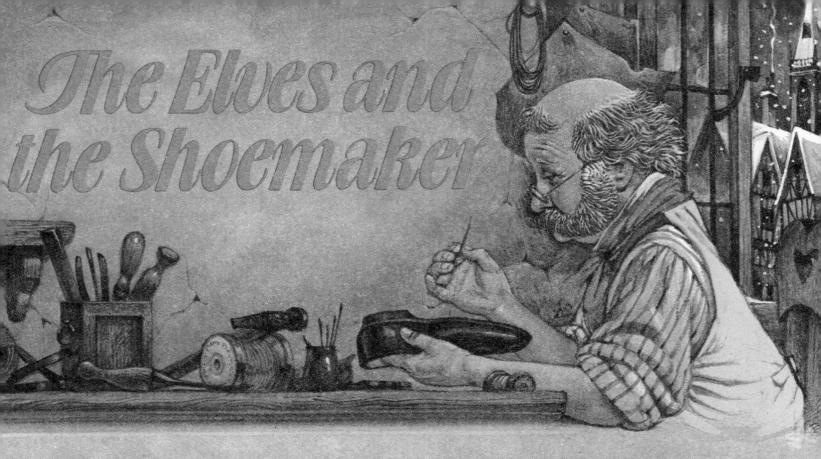

The Elves and the Shoemaker

"Can't you work any faster, my dear?" said the shoemaker's wife anxiously.

The shoemaker smiled: "Oh, I *could* work faster," he said. "I could cut out the leather for my shoes less neatly, and I could sew with bigger stitches. But I like to give the customers my very best workmanship. And that takes time."

"I know, dear, but there's no money left over to buy more leather. You work so carefully that it takes you two days to make one pair of shoes."

"I'm doing my best," said the shoemaker sadly. "My eyesight isn't as good as it was and my fingers aren't so quick."

The shoemaker continued to do his slow, careful best. But there was soon no money left to buy leather, and all his hides and suedes were used up. Only one scrap of leather was left on his workbench.

"What shall we do tomorrow when there's no leather to sew and when there are no more shoes to sell?" asked his wife.

The shoemaker smiled. "Well, let's worry about that tomorrow."

He spent all day cutting out a pair of shoes from the last of the leather. "These are probably the last shoes I shall ever make," he thought, "so they must be my best."

When he went to bed, he left the cut-out shapes on his workbench.

"I'm sorry we are so poor, my dear," he said to his wife as he climbed into bed.

"You can only do your best," she said comfortingly. "You can't do any more."

down to the tags on their laces.

"What craftsmanship!" said the shoemaker to his wife. The shoes brought such a good price that this time he was able to buy enough leather for *four* pairs of shoes. And the next night, the mysterious visitors sewed all four pairs.

"Such perfect cobbling!" exclaimed the customers. And they came from miles around to buy the shoemaker's wares. There were long, glossy riding boots for the men and pretty velvet dancing shoes for the ladies.

"We have enough leather for a lifetime!" said the shoemaker's happy wife. "And so many people come here to buy their shoes that we are almost *rich*!"

But the shoemaker was thinking. "Wouldn't you like to know who is helping us every night? It's time we found out."

So one cold night, just before Christmas, the shoemaker left the cut-out leather on his workbench, then he and his wife hid nearby.

As midnight struck, out from behind the clock crept six naked little elves. They climbed on to the bench and went to work at once, sewing and hammering and

In the morning, the shoemaker cleaned his glasses and threaded his needle and looked around for the pieces of leather. But something *amazing* had happened. A finished pair of shoes stood in the centre of the bench, perfect to the last shiny buckle. Someone had made the shoes for him, overnight.

"Just look at the workmanship!" he exclaimed, showing them to his wife. "And look at the beautiful tiny stitches! Who could have made them?"

The shoes were so well made that they sold for twice the usual price. So the old shoemaker was able to buy a new strip of leather and cut out *two* pairs of shoes during the day. At night he left the cut-out shapes on his workbench and went to bed a much more cheerful man.

In the morning, the two pairs of shoes were completely finished, right

lacing and polishing. Every now and then they stopped to blow into their cold hands or stamp their cold feet or hug themselves against the chilly night air. They were shivering blue from head to foot.

"Poor little mites," said the shoemaker's wife. "All that work for us and they haven't got a shirt or even a pair of boots."

"Well, after all they've done for us, we ought to give them a thank-you present," said the shoemaker.

The next day his wife was soon busy cutting out little shirts and trousers from some bright warm cloth. The shoemaker took out his finest needle and softest leather and made a handsome pair of boots for each elf.

On Christmas night, they left their presents on the workbench and hid as they had done before. It was bitterly cold. When the six little elves appeared, they were shuddering and shivering, and their breath turned white in the frosty air.

They were confused at first, when they could find no boot leather to sew. But when they saw the clothes and realised that they were for them, they put them on and danced about, laughing and clapping their hands inside their new woolly mittens.

"No more cobbling for us! We're smart fellows now!" And they all sang as they danced out of the shop and down the street.

"So! No more help from the elves," said the shoemaker's wife, laughing. "How will you manage now that so many people come to you for their shoes and boots?"

The shoemaker smiled. "I'll just have to do my best," he said.

"I'm sure you will, my dear," said his wife.

"You always do."

SNOW WHITE
and the
seven dwarfs

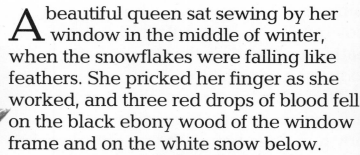

A beautiful queen sat sewing by her window in the middle of winter, when the snowflakes were falling like feathers. She pricked her finger as she worked, and three red drops of blood fell on the black ebony wood of the window frame and on the white snow below.

"I wish for a daughter with skin as white as snow, lips as red as blood and hair as black as ebony," she sighed.

And so it happened. She had a little girl with skin as white as snow, with lips as red as blood and with hair as black as ebony. Her parents called her Snow White. But only a few days after her birth, her mother died.

Her father, the king, had truly loved his queen, but he needed a mother for Snow White, so he searched for a second wife.

He married a princess whose face was lovely as summer, but her heart was cold as ice and she worked dark magic. She was so vain she could not bear to think that anyone could be more beautiful than she was. When she came to the palace, the only thing she brought was a mirror in a golden frame. Each night, she whispered:

"Mirror, mirror, on the wall,
Who is the fairest one of all?"

And the mirror would answer:
"You, O Queen, are the fairest one by far!"

This made the new queen very happy, for she knew that the mirror could not lie. She preened herself in front of the glass and smiled in satisfaction.

But Snow White grew more and more beautiful every year until, one day, when she was seven, her wicked stepmother asked her usual question:

"Mirror, mirror, on the wall,
Who is the fairest one of all?"
This time the mirror replied:

"You, O Queen, are fair, and lovely too,
But Snow White is more fair than you!"
The queen was furious, and her lovely face turned ugly with rage. She called for her huntsman. "Take Snow White into the forest and kill her!" she screamed. "Cut out her heart and bring it to me as proof that you have done as I have ordered!"

Pale and trembling, the royal huntsman found Snow White playing in the garden, and grabbed her by the hand. Not once did he look at her. Not once did he speak.

Deep in the forest, he drew his dagger and held it to Snow White's heart. "Now you must die!"

But when she looked up at him, her red lips trembled and her black hair spilled around her shoulders.

"Let the wild beasts kill you," cried the huntsman. "I cannot!" And he ran off, leaving her alone in the forest.

On his way back to the palace, he killed a small fallow deer and cut out its heart. When he gave it to the cruel queen, he told her it was Snow White's heart. She gave a wild laugh and threw it to her dogs. "So much for Snow White!" she cried.

Snow White wandered lonely through the forest, frightened at shadows and fearful of strange sounds. But when the trees and bushes saw how lovely and afraid she was, they turned aside their thorns, and the sharp stones refused to cut her feet.

At dusk, she found a tiny house among the trees. There was no answer to her knock, so she pushed the door and went in.

What a funny little place it was! Everything was very neat. There was a checked cloth spread on the table, with seven loaves, and seven plates, seven knives, forks, spoons and goblets of wine, all laid out ready for supper. By the wall, there were seven beds, all in a row.

"I'm very hungry," thought Snow White, and she took a small bite from each piece of bread and then a sip of wine from each goblet. Then she tried each bed in turn.

"This bed is too long," she said, ". . . and this one is too short." But when she

20

reached the seventh bed, it was just right. Soon, she was fast asleep.

The seven dwarfs who lived in the cottage returned at nightfall. They had been digging for gold in the mountains and were tired after their long day's work. They lit their candles and looked around the room.

"Who's been sitting on my stool?" said the first dwarf.

"And touching my plate?"

"And eating my bread?"

"And licking my spoon?"

"And using my fork?"

"And moving my knife?"

"And drinking my wine?" said the seventh and last dwarf.

The first dwarf went over to the bed by the wall. "Someone has been lying in my bed," he cried.

"And mine! And mine!" said the others.

"There is someone still sleeping in my bed," said the seventh and last dwarf.

They crowded round the bed to look.

"Less noise!" said the first dwarf.

"Keep those lights down!" said the second.

"Be careful not to wake her!" said the third.

So the last dwarf slept the night with the others, an hour in each bed.

with rage, and she screamed in fury as she demanded where Snow White could be found.

The mirror sighed heavily and told her.

Disguising herself as a pedlar, the wicked queen searched the forest until she found the cottage.

"Fine wares to sell!" she cried, as she knocked at the little door.

"Good morning," said Snow White. "Do you have some pretty things for me to buy?"

"I have laces, bobbins and ribbons of every colour of the rainbow," said the queen.

Snow White quite forgot the dwarfs' solemn warning as she let the visitor in.

"Gracious, child," the queen exclaimed. "How badly your bodice is

Snow White was very frightened when she woke up next morning and saw the dwarfs, but they listened to her story and were delighted she had come to stay.

"You can cook, can't you?" asked the first dwarf.

"And wash? And clean, and knit and spin?" asked the others.

"Then of course you must live with us," they chorused. "But remember — don't let anyone into the house while we are away."

For months, the queen thought that Snow White was dead, and she did not ask the mirror her question again until late one evening, when the king was away.

"*Mirror, mirror, on the wall,*
 Who is the fairest one of all?"
   The mirror replied:
"*You, O Queen, are fair, and lovely*
   too,
But Snow White's still more fair than
   you."
   The queen's face turned black

laced! Let me do it," and she took a ribbon from her tray.

The pedlar threaded the ribbon, then pulled it tighter and tighter until the breath was squeezed out of Snow White's body and she fell down in a faint.

"So much for your beauty!" cackled the cruel queen. "Now you will die!"

"We're home!" called the dwarfs. But no-one answered. Snow White was as pale as death when they found her.

"Loosen her lace!" the dwarfs shouted in panic. When the first dwarf cut it, the life-giving air rushed into her lungs and Snow White quickly recovered.

"The queen will find out you're alive," they warned. "You mustn't let her in."

Of course, the queen soon found out that Snow White was not dead. Using all her magic powers, she prepared a very special apple. One side was green and safe to eat, the other side was red — and deadly poisonous.

"Apples!" she called, knocking at the cottage door. "Crisp, juicy apples!"

"Please go away," Snow White said,

as she peeped through the window. "I'm not allowed to open the door to strangers."

"Wise girl," replied the queen as she took the poisoned apple from her basket and turned the green side to her lips to bite into it. "Here," she said. "Take the rest and enjoy it."

The apple did look extremely good. Snow White leaned out of the window and took the half which was red and juicy. She took one bite . . . and fell down dead.

"That's the end of you!" chortled the queen as she returned home in triumph.

At nightfall, the dwarfs came back from the mountain. "No!" cried the first dwarf, when he found Snow White.

23

"How empty our lives will be without her," they all said sorrowfully.

The dwarfs could not bury her in the cold dark earth, so they made a coffin of glass so that they could still see her. Then they made a golden plaque and wrote on it:

"Here lies Snow White, the daughter of a king."

They set the coffin on a green hill and guarded it day and night. Birds came to sing there. And animals came to sit there. The squirrels came first, then the rabbits and last a young fallow deer.

Snow White lay in her coffin for many years, and never once did the dwarfs leave her alone. Slowly she grew into a young woman, more beautiful than she had ever been.

At last a prince rode past and saw the coffin and the words written on the golden plaque.

"I would like to take her away with me," he said, but the dwarfs would not part with her.

"Will you take money?" he asked.

"She was worth more to us than all the gold in the world," the dwarfs replied.

"Then for sheer pity, let me kiss her once!" begged the prince. "For if she were alive, I would have loved her more than life itself!"

The dwarfs talked among themselves. "All right, just one kiss," they

said, and opened the glass coffin.

But as the prince's lips touched the lips of Snow White, a piece of apple fell from her mouth and she opened her eyes.

"Where am I?"

"Safe," said the prince. And when Snow White looked into his face she could hardly believe what she saw.

"Your eyes are the colour of the sea. Your hair is as golden as the sun!"

The prince was overjoyed as he lifted her from the coffin. "I love you more than all the world. Marry me, and come with me to my father's kingdom."

And so Snow White said goodbye to the seven dwarfs, who had loved her so much. She thanked them, and promised that she would visit them often. Then she went with the prince to his father's castle where a great feast was prepared for their wedding.

Meanwhile the wicked queen preened herself in front of the magic mirror.

*"Mirror, mirror, on the wall,
Who is the fairest one of all?"*

The mirror gave a triumphant laugh:
*"Your loathsome face is black as night,
Compared to the beauty of Snow White!"*

"Aaargh!" screamed the queen, and tore the mirror off the wall and dashed it against the window sill. It shattered into a thousand pieces. A sliver of glass, as sharp as an icicle, pierced the queen's wicked heart and she fell down dead among the glittering fragments.

So the wicked queen never lived to see Snow White at her loveliest — riding at her father's side to her wedding in the palace chapel where her handsome prince awaited her.

Peter and the Mountainy Men

Long, long ago, in the mountains of Switzerland, there lived a rich miller who was very mean. Even when people were starving and pleading for food, he would not help them.

One cold winter's day there was a knock on the mill door. "What do you want?" barked the miller.

"Please, sir, could you give me just one small bag of flour?" pleaded a tiny man dressed in a red cap and little green suit. "We need it so badly."

"Buzz off!" shouted the miller. "I've no time for beggars!"

As the dwarf began his long walk back to the mountains, he met a young boy carrying a bag of flour in his arms. It was Peter, the miller's son.

"Take this," he whispered, "but don't let my father know I've given it to you."

The dwarf took the bag and tucked it inside his coat. "Thank you, young sir," he said. "I'll not forget your kindness." Then he continued on his way.

One spring morning, several months

later, Peter was fishing in a lake up in the mountains when he felt a strong pull on his line. He tugged and tugged, until suddenly, a little figure appeared from out of the water. It was the dwarf!

"Why, if it isn't the miller's son!" he said, drying himself on a huge leaf. "I've been having my annual bath in honour of the Great Day."

"Great Day?" asked Peter.

"Didn't you know? Today's our Great Day of Feasts and Sports. Why don't you come and join us? It's great fun and there's heaps to eat!"

The dwarf dived into the long grass, and pulled out his red cap and green clothes. Then he led the way through a hollow tree trunk to a huge cave in the hillside. This was where all the mountainy people — the elves, the dwarfs and the fairies — make their home.

In the huge cave hundreds of little folk dressed in gaily coloured clothes sat at long, low tables munching cakes, jellies and ice-cream. And there were great bowls of fruit and tall jugs of juice.

The dwarf banged on the table for silence. Immediately the chattering and music stopped.

"Dwarfs, goblins and fairies, this is Peter, the boy who gave us the bag of flour last winter. He's here as my special guest for the Great Day!"

The mountainy people clapped and cheered, as Peter sat down at the head table and began to eat, and eat . . . and eat. But, long before he had finished, the games began.

There was hurdling over the benches and pole-vaulting over the tables. The leprechauns played shinty, and a big crowd gathered to watch the darts match played with goose feathers. Skittles were played with a marble and big fir cones, and for javelin-throwing they used long twigs.

Peter was invited to join in the fun, but refused politely. "I don't really think it would be fair. After all, I'm so much bigger than you . . . and stronger."

"I wouldn't count on that," said a goblin — and he lifted up the bench, Peter and all!

The miller's son sat entranced as the elves rode bareback on racing mice, and the fairies used little wooden boats to race down a stream running through the cave. And all the time there were dwarfs doing handstands and somersaults, sometimes for prizes but mostly for fun. Then, after a tug-of-war between the goblins and the

gremlins, everyone ran out to the top of the mountain and back — and fell down exhausted.

Peter picked his way through the tired little bodies, taking care not to step on the fairies' wings. He crept out of the cave and climbed up the tree trunk back to the lake.

Just as he picked up his fishing rod he heard a voice calling to him. "Wait, Peter, wait for me!" It was the mountainy man. "You're leaving without your presents."

"Presents? But it isn't my birthday."

"I know it isn't. I mean your thank-you presents. You gave us flour when we were starving, so please take this whistle in return for your kindness. Just blow it loudly three times and we"ll bring you whatever you want."

Amazed at all he had seen, Peter could scarcely find words to thank the little man. "And this," said the dwarf taking a bag from inside his coat, "is a flour bag for your father."

As the sun was sinking, Peter reached the mill, gave his father the bag and told him that the dwarf had given it to him.

"You mean you sneaked out and gave one of my bags of flour to that little beggar?" shouted the miller. But then he peeped inside the bag . . . and found a hundred shining pearls, with a note:

We hope this makes you happy not sad,
Mountainy folk return good for bad.

The miller felt so ashamed he promised Peter that never again would he turn away anyone in need of help.

So, ever after that, when the first winter snow fell high on the mountains, all the little people visited their friends, the miller and Peter.

And they always found the miller's table laden with delicious food.